When Abe Met Lane

The Other Lane

Marla Holt

Published by Marla Holt, 2018.

To Anna, for your endless encouragement and support.
You are an inspiration.

To Find out more and for exclusive sneak peeks at Marla's newest work,
<u>sign up for her newsletter</u>[1]

• • • •

Keep Reading for the first chapter of
The Other Lane: A Modern Fairy Tale
Available Now

---

1. https://mailchi.mp/fa479f9eea16/when-abe-met-lane

Acknowledgements

This book is one hundred per cent the result of a loving family and encouraging and vibrant online writing community. If we've connected on Ravelry, on Instagram, on Facebook, or any other social network, thank you. I couldn't have written this book without you.

Thank you especially to my husband, Brock, who reads every draft of every story, who encourages me daily, and who lets me take all the naps. I love you.

E very day for the past week, Abe had told himself he would not to go back to Cristo's Coffee.

The owner of the little, out of the way shop had called him the week before. He had deep pockets and wanted to sell beer and wine and the occasional Irish coffee alongside his lattes and sandwiches. Abe couldn't do much for the man since he also owned the liquor store next door. Kansas's liquor laws were strict about who could sell alcohol by the glass. Even if he purchased his booze from another supplier, the state wouldn't grant him a license. The laws were what the man wanted changed, and since Abe worked for the liquor lobby, he was about the only person to call. Abe had told the man to prepare for a long, frustrating fight. He'd been at it for almost fifteen years, and had barely made any progress.

It was the end of January, only two weeks into this year's leg-islative session, so the time was good. The more support Abe's firm garnered for expanding liquor laws in Kansas, the more headway he could clear for the large grocery store chains to sell liquor in their stores. The coffee shop owner's investment loaned a much-needed backing from a local business.

When Abe had visited Cristo's again the day after his first meeting there, he'd told himself it was because he'd enjoyed the coffee.

The coffee had been phenomenal.

But the shop had been different on his second visit. There had been a different woman behind the counter. She had been younger than the one he'd wanted to see. This bored red head had not been the black-haired beauty with the wide pink smile and curvy hips Abe had wanted to wrap his fingers around.

Abe had sighed with both relief and disappointment when the black-haired woman hadn't been there. She'd been pretty, but he shouldn't to indulge an attraction with a woman so much younger than him.

Abe had told himself twice. Then he'd bought a cup of lukewarm coffee and told himself he wasn't going back.

But he could not get her black hair out of his head.

It didn't matter how many times he told himself she was too young. He wanted to see her again. He *needed* to see her again.

She had to be at least twenty-five, right?

Abe had turned forty-two at the beginning of January. Twenty-five-year-olds hadn't been appealing to him since he was in his early thirties, but he couldn't forget the woman's smiling face and assessing, clever blue eyes.

He'd kept his distance over the weekend, despite the flier he'd seen advertising a Sunday brunch. Abe and Gretchen went to their usual brunch place that Sunday He needed a better reason than interest in a new woman to change up his routine with his daughter. Gretchen looked forward to the waffles at Paradox every week, and he strove to never disappoint his daughter.

Abe tried to list out the reasons why he shouldn't pursue the black-haired barista. Aside from age, all he could come up with was that he hadn't been single that long.

Sure, his marriage had ended over ten years ago, but it had only been six weeks since he and Nicole had split. Surely, he needed more time to mourn the end of a relationship that had lasted almost a year.

Except that he didn't.

Abe had told Nicole it was over after Thanksgiving, because she'd been dropping hints about rings and asking subtle questions about their future. Even though Abe had yearned for a partner, for a house full of children, his favorite thing about Nicole had been waking up at her house and having breakfast with her eleven-year-old son.

That wasn't a good basis for a long-term relationship. Besides that, Gretchen had hated Nicole. She'd never gone farther than saying, "Dad, she's a Slytherin," but the implications had been clear.

As he pulled into the last open spot in front of Cristo's on Tuesday, Abe wondered what House Gretchen would sort the woman from the coffee shop into. She was the reason for his third visit in a week.

He should have at least asked the legislator at the top of his list to come along with him, maybe even a few others just to show them it wasn't all national grocery chains vying for the changes. But if Abe invited anyone, he would have to work. He knew he shouldn't talk to her, but that didn't change that she was the reason he was there.

It had been hard enough to shrug Jeff, his best friend and colleague, off. If Abe wasn't wooing elected officials, he was strategizing with Jeff. And though he'd told Jeff he was checking in with the coffee shop owner, that he didn't want to get the man's hopes up if the both of them showed up, Jeff had raised his eyebrows and rolled his lips between his teeth.

"And the girl?" Jeff had asked, because Abe had been stupid enough to mention he thought the barista was pretty after their first visit.

Abe shrugged, and said, "This is business." He'd wanted to correct Jeff, but if he pointed out the barista was a woman, not a girl, it would giveaway that he was lying.

Cristo's patrons already knew the secret of the black-haired barista. Every table was full when he strolled in. There had only been two or three other people while the red head had been working. The dull roar of conversation buzzed over the top of contemporary jazz, and sure enough, there she stood, behind the bar, scrubbing the counter where she'd pulled out the wire syrup racks.

The only place left to sit was at the bar, so Abe pulled out a stool and sat. He wore his best charcoal suit, cut to show off his athletic figure. Abe knew women found him attractive, but as the barista turned and scanned him, he'd never been more conscious of the silver hair at his temples or the wrinkles by the corners of his eyes.

Her gaze snagged below his eye level. The fire behind her blue eyes blazed at something familiar. Did she recognize his tie? He saw her mind categorizing him based on his wardrobe. Her own attire spoke of someone who worked a minimum wage job. She wore scarred skinny jeans with a whole over one knee, scuffed boots that came to mid-calf, and a red flannel shirt she'd tied up at her waist revealing a hint of belly button as she moved.

She wasn't thin, but the roundness of her hips and stomach were proportionate to her chest and shoulders, and the way she'd tied her shirt only emphasized the pleasing dip of her waist. Abe thought of mid-century pinup girls when he looked at her but couldn't imagine her posing sweetly in red bikini. This woman was fire, he felt it from where he sat, and she was not impressed with him.

He was so busy assessing her thoughts about him, Abe almost missed her asking him if he needed anything. A full second passed before he reigned himself back in enough to say, "Just a cup of drip."

She squinted at him, once again, her eyes on his chest. "Is that for here or to go, Abraham Fujikawa?"

He tugged the ugly red name tag free and tucked it into an inner pocket. He forced his smile wider even as he burned with embarrassment on the inside.

"For here," he said, and then to make himself sound more impressive than a dork who wore a name tag everywhere, he added, "And it's just Abe. I came straight from the Statehouse."

"The Statehouse at this time of year?" She arched her delicate black eyebrows, "Does that mean you're a lobbyist?"

He held his shoulders back and puffed out his chest. He was so used to slouching, making himself look smaller because people didn't expect an Asian man to be tall, that he sometimes forgot he was doing it. "It does."

She turned around to warm up a mug for him. Abe almost felt guilty about watching her hips as she moved but couldn't stop imagining how soft and full she would feel beneath his hands. "I always forget how many of you there are in this city." She handed him the mug. "But then January arrives and you all swarm out of the woodwork like cockroaches."

Abe stifled a laugh as he rose to fill his mug from the air pots stationed at the other end of the counter. "You don't like lobbyists."

"Most of the time, no."

Her eyes trailed him as walked, and a familiar satisfaction settled in as he hoped she liked what she saw.

That blue fire was assessing his suit again as he returned. "Unless you're advocating more funding for schools or expanding Medicare or something altruistic." The implication was he didn't fit the model, because someone more altruistic would give their money to those less fortunate instead of spending it on expensive clothes.

"I can't claim anything that magnanimous," Abe admitted as he sat down again. "I work with people like your boss to loosen up the liquor laws."

"The legislators you work with understand words that big?"

There was that fire coming out.

"You forgot to put on your 'Liberal and Proud' button on this morning."

She smirked at him, and a flame seared deep into his chest. "Not the kind of company you usually keep?"

He shrugged, not hinting at the way the heat from her flame made the raging squall living inside him calm into a series of cascading waves playing in a warm summer breeze. "I care more about passing legislation than political party."

The barista did not look impressed, even as she watched him swallow a mouthful of light roast.

"How noble," she said. "Is that what brings you here straight from the Statehouse? I can call Randy."

Oh hell no, she was not passing him off to her boss. Not now.

"Today I just came for you." Abe let his smile turn a little wolfish.

"Jesus." she stepped back and frowned at him. "Tone it down a little. I'm a captive audience."

"I meant, you're the only one around here who makes good coffee," he switched tack, trading the salacious smile for a more neutral one.

"It's true, I leave for school and the quality of service goes to shit."

"That must be why this stool is always occupied. You have a following."

"The demographic that occupies that stool generally isn't all that interested in the quality of my coffee." She adjusted the cuff of her sleeve.

"Why is that?" Abe asked.

"You tell me."

Well damn. "Am I fitting into your usual demographic?"

She looked him up and down again. "Let's see. Forties. Business Attire. You don't wear a wedding band, so you're divorced, probably with a kid or two, most likely with an ex-wife you wouldn't mind pissing off by dating someone half her age."

"Am I that transparent?"

"You are one of many, my friend."

"I'm not trying piss off my ex-wife."

"Then you have a healthier mindset than most."

"Or I've been divorced longer." Abe changed the subject. His divorce wasn't something he talked about. "What are you studying?"

"I'm finishing up my BFA in textiles, and I do some work in ceramics."

He should have known she was a fellow artist. He also boasted a Bachelor of Fine Arts, but he wouldn't tell her in what. Not when she would just assume he was making it up to impress her. "Of course, what do you make?"

"Fabric and pots."

"I had guessed that much, believe it or not."

She sighed and the edge to her voice annoyed. "My emphases are in complex knitting and Japanese ceramic forms."

Abe hadn't been to mass since he found his wife in bed with another man, hadn't believed in God for a long time before that, but he almost crossed himself in relief at this one tenuous connection.

"Now see, if you were studying Japanese, I could help," he said, "but the only thing I know about Japanese pottery is how to drink sake out of it."

"I don't need your help," she said with a flat voice. "I'm in my last semester. I've got my technique down pretty well by now."

"I never said you didn't, I was just—"

"You were just showing off."

He gave her his best half grin. "Was it working?"

And she shot him down with unveiled disdain. "I'm supposed to be impressed that a Japanese man speaks the language? Come back when you're fluent in Dutch or something."

"You don't like me," Abe said as he stood for a refill. She watched him again as he walked the few feet to the end of the counter and emptied the last of the light roast into his mug. She crossed to the grinder and weighed out beans as if it were an automatic response to the sound of the spluttering air pot.

As Abe watched her prepare the coffee, he wondered how long she'd worked in coffee shops. The older gentleman who spoke to her as he filled his mug with decaf seemed to like her. She even smiled at him. What would it take for Abe to make her smile?

"Don't take it personally," she said upon her return. "If you sit on that stool, it's predetermined that I won't like you."

"What if tomorrow I came in and sat on this stool?" he patted the cushion next to him.

"Then I'm sure Allison would serve you a weak, cold cup of coffee and ignore you while checking Facebook on her phone."

Allison must be the red head.

"Why don't you ignore me too?"

She cocked her head to the side, squinting at him in a way that told him he wasn't all that bright. "Because it's bad for tips to ignore the customers, and the wages here suck."

"You flirt with people for money?"

She motioned between the two of them with a huff. "I wouldn't exactly call this flirting."

"But you do?" He asked again.

"It's not like I'm bribing elected officials on behalf of someone with deep pockets, I've got to eat."

That was a heavy indictment. "Is that what you think I do?"

She gave him a sweet, mocking smile, not at all like the one she'd given the old man. "Me calling you corrupt is about as flattering as you calling me an emotional prostitute, don't you think?"

"I'm sorry," Abe stood, and perhaps it was the brittle note in his apology, or maybe it was that she was so short he loomed over her as he leaned over the counter, but she stiffened and backed up a step. "We should start over," Abe said in a gentle voice, then held out his hand. "I'm Abe Fujikawa, and you make a damn fine cup of coffee."

She stared at his hand for a few seconds, before uncrossing her arms and giving him one firm, short shake. Her hand was dry and calloused. Not smooth and dainty like most women.

"I'm Lane," she said as she stepped out of his reach. But he swore she was reevaluating him.

"That wasn't so bad, was it?" he asked.

Lane shrugged. "It could have been worse. Points for the *Twin Peaks* reference though."

He let out the chuckle that rose in his throat. "How much do I owe you for the coffee?"

"It's an even two."

Abe pulled too many bills from his wallet and laid them on the counter. "I'll see you Thursday, Lane," he said, then didn't give her a chance to respond before retreating.

Chapter Two

It was his stupidest hang up, but as he passed his still unfinished bedroom, he closed the door. He needed to pretend the mess inside wasn't there as he worked on the little bedroom across the hall.

There were four bedrooms in the house, all of them upstairs. He'd finished Gretchen's first. He'd made the upstairs flooring and duct work a priority when he'd moved in ten years ago just so Gretchen had her own space in his house. Her room remained the only finished one in the entire remodel. He'd even redecorated it as her Christmas present this year, because on her fourteenth birthday she'd told him she'd outgrown princess pink. Now her bedroom was a sleek mint green with white and gold accents.

After Gretchen's room, Abe had finished the guest room. It was a smaller room at the end of the hall where his dad stayed a few times a year. Comfortable with a handmade quilt on the bed and a overstuffed old armchair in the corner, it would have made an ideal space for Abe to sleep while he finished his own bedroom, but he had never used it.

No, after ten years, Abe still slept on a futon in the living room which he rolled up every morning and hid in the hall closet like he was still living in his tiny Tokyo apartment.

It wasn't like it would take much work to finish his bedroom. The bedroom floor had long been finished. The wiring and plumbing for the bathroom needed a professional's hand, but the tub was in the barn waiting for installation. The tile too. The walls were up, but still needed mudded and taped, then painted.

It wasn't like he was *that* far behind. He had worked on the bedroom here and there over the years, but he was in no hurry to finish it.

For now, Abe used the room as a storage area. The power tools and saw horses, the drop cloths and plastic all lived in his unfinished bedroom to keep the rest of the house neat and dust free. The dust part didn't work, but it helped his peace of mind that the rest of the house wasn't littered with tools.

Abe liked things neat. Organized. Clean.

He never left dishes in the sink. He swept the living room and kitchen every night before bed. He dusted the house from top to bottom every Saturday night when he finished with his building for the day.

That was another reason why, after ten years, his house wasn't finished yet. He did most of the work himself. Sometimes his friends helped. But there was only so much you got done with just Jeff and Bryce's occasional help. They were more suppliers of good beer than real help, despite Bryce's contracting license. Work took up sixty hours of his week, and Sundays were for Gretchen. Then there was tennis, and sleep, and, if he was lucky, a date on Friday night—which left Saturdays for the house.

And it was a big house.

Abe had moved into the huge, dilapidated farmhouse two years after he'd moved out of Roxanne's place. The divorce had just been settled and the townhouse he'd been living in had reminded him too much of his state of mind since then.

Generic.

Vacant.

Transient.

He'd lived in a fog for months, still in shock from coming home to find his wife in bed with a man she worked with at her law firm while their three-year-old daughter slept next door.

Anger and outrage still swelled beneath his skin like waves stirring to meet a squall when he thought of that night. Abe had thought his and Roxanne's marriage had been a good one. Five years in, they'd had their differences, but overall, they had been making things work—at least he had thought so. Roxanne never had given him a good reason for how he'd failed. Just that Greg could give her things he couldn't.

Greg. A man who was overweight and balding, but who had more money and more influence than Abe ever would. Greg, who was a good Catholic. Greg, who'd never done a lick of real work in his life, but ridden his father's coattails through law school and into his father's law firm. And thank goodness Abe and Roxanne had been married at the courthouse on impulse so The Church could pretend Roxanne had never been married before.

Abe never would understand it, but it wasn't his problem anymore. Roxanne had made the life she wanted. She still lived in the house they'd bought together, the one they could barely afford back then, but he was sure Greg's money had paid off by now. She and Greg had two sons, and Gretchen lived with them most of the week. That was the part that still broke his heart. One day a week with the person he loved most in the world because he'd reacted poorly to a shitty situation.

Abe had learned not to dwell on his past early on, and projects like renovating this giant, old, empty house kept him preoccupied. Even if Abe avoided finishing his bedroom because he didn't want to sleep there alone.

He should have had a partner by now. Someone to share the space with, someone fill the house with enough kids to warrant the four bedrooms and giant farmhouse table in the dining room. But things hadn't worked out with Nicole, and Lane, the pretty barista wasn't interested.

Abe had returned to Cristo's that next Thursday to see Lane. She'd been nice. Well, as nice as she could be. She hadn't cursed at him or called him a cockroach, but she hadn't exactly welcomed him either.

He'd sat down on the same stool and when she'd turned around from making a latte to see him there, she'd paused and blinked.

"You came back."

Abe had winked at her and said, "I don't scare easy."

She'd snorted. "Apparently. Black coffee for here?"

Abe had nodded and unfolded his newspaper while she'd fetched him a mug. The morning rush picked up, and she and the redheaded barista had been too busy helping customers to pay him much attention. It wasn't until Abe had been counting out bills to pay for his coffee that Lane intercepted him. She'd pulled the money from between his fingers, counted out enough to cover the coffee, plus a dollar, then crumpled the rest in her fist and thrust it back into his hand.

"Don't tip so much. It makes you look desperate," was all she'd said before she'd turned her back on him.

Most of their interactions for the past month had been similar.

So yes, she was not interested. With zero prospects on the horizon and no energy to go out looking, Abe avoided finishing his bedroom again. Instead, he worked on the only room that was still little more than studs and flooring. It was the smallest room in the house, but also closest to the master bedroom, and that made it even more painful to work on than his bedroom.

Abe had always imagined he'd finish this room while awaiting the arrival his next child. Then it would be there waiting for the child after that. If he was lucky, he'd have a fourth. But lately, he wondered if it was even worth the bother of building a nursery.

Forty-two was late in life to start another family.

As he gathered the wood he needed to frame out a closet in a room where there had never been one, he tried to think of working on the nursery today as a sign he remained hopeful. A wife and a family could still be out there waiting for him somewhere.

When five o'clock rolled around, he was covered in sawdust and wood glue and had smashed him thumb twice. Jeff had invited him to have dinner with the family and watch the basketball game, so Abe was about ready to pack it in when his phone pinged with a text in his pocket—his first all day.

Gretchen: *Mom says I have to go to mass tomorrow.*

This was not a new argument, and Abe sighed.

Abe: *Why aren't you going tonight?*

Gretchen: *Because I'm going to the movies with Maddy.*

Abe: *I guess you better get up early tomorrow then.*

Gretchen: *Or you could take me and we can go to brunch afterward?*

Abe: *Nice try.*

Gretchen: *Come, on. Pleeeeeease.*

Abe: *Sorry, Sweetie. It's your mom's rule, and it's your responsibility to follow it.*

Gretchen: *How about we don't go to church and just tell Mom we did?*

Abe: *Are you suggesting you'd lie to your mother?*

Gretchen: *You would be the one lying, I'd be the one not saying anything in the background.*

Abe: *Absolutely not.*

Gretchen: *But I don't want to go to church anymore.*

Abe: *Either skip the movies or get up early tomorrow. Your choice.*

Gretchen: *If I lived with you, you wouldn't make me go to church.*

Abe: *But your mom still would.*

Abe watched as the little three dots stopped and started a few times before Gretchen's text finally came through.

Gretchen: *Fine, but the second I turn 18, I quit.*

Abe: *I'll pick you up from the church at 10. I found a
new place to try for brunch.*

Gretchen's only reply was an emoji sticking its tongue out at
him.

He hated upholding Roxanne's rules, especially the ones he'd
railed against in his own youth, but he wasn't about to put
Gretchen in the middle of a disagreement like that. There were
things Abe would go to the mat on but arguing about church was
not one of them. Nothing about the situation hurt his daughter, and she didn't see it now, but if she wanted to leave the
church once she was an adult, she'd be surer of her convictions.
And she'd have the pain of still having to attend a Catholic high
school out of the way. The one thing Abe and Roxanne agreed
on: Gretchen would go to the best school in town, no matter the
cost. Abe happily paid the tuition.

That part about brunch? Cristo's had not been a part of his
Sunday plans. He'd planned to go to the waffle bar at Paradox as
always. It was their thing, but the hopefulness from working on
the nursery personified itself in the form of a short, black haired
woman with fire burning in her blue eyes, and how delicious she
would look with her stomach rounded with his child.

He'd indulged in the fantasy of it all day as he'd worked, but
now cut it off as absurd. He thought she might be closer to thirty
than twenty, but it was hard to tell, and he wasn't rude enough
to ask. Lane could be twenty-two for all he knew.

And Abe didn't like younger women—not that much
younger anyway.

But that didn't stop him from imagining how soft her skin would be beneath his fingers.

Chapter Three

Cristo's was busier than Abe had ever seen it. Groups crowded in around tables cluttered with too many dishes. Steam looped up from behind open newspapers from individuals who lingered on the plush furniture. Abe and Gretchen secured seats at a tiny bistro table by the front windows after an older couple left. Lane rushed over to bus the table with a quick, "Hey," to him and a sidelong glance at Gretchen while she cleaned. Then she was gone again, attending to the line at the register.

"What do you think everyone likes so much?" Gretchen asked as they waited their turn in line. "It doesn't even look like they have waffles."

"Give it a chance," he said. "The coffee's fantastic."

Gretchen turned in a circle, surveying the crowd around them. "Everybody is eating cinnamon rolls," she said as they moved forward one step in line.

"Then we should try the cinnamon rolls." He slung an arm around her shoulder, and she didn't shrug him off, which he counted as a win. His daughter wasn't embarrassed to be seen with him in public, but she wasn't always keen on affection either.

His need to touch those he loved in public was probably the most obviously American thing about him—that and the beard. Abe had worn a beard for the last thirteen years. Twenty-seven and just out of law school was young for a lobbyist. With the beard, Abe hadn't looked so young or so much like the actor he'd once tried to be. When he visited Japan with his dad, the beard was the first marker he wasn't Japanese.

Only two more years and Gretchen would accompany them on their yearly trip to Tokyo. There was a whole half of her family that Gretchen didn't know because her mother was afraid Gretchen would go away and never come back.

But Gretchen was a Fujikawa, and Roxanne had forgotten that Fujikawas were loyal to a fault. Abe's father had worked hard to keep his ties with the family that never came to see them. It had been a rift for decades, that Abe's father and mother moved to the states at all. But when you were a nuclear physicist in the 1960s, the United States was the place to be. Then Abe was born in the States, and none of the many job offers that had come his father's way in the decades since their immigration had tempted him back.

"I'm old," Abe's father would say. "I've lived here for half my life. My wife is buried here. My son is here. My granddaughter. This is home."

Abe agreed.

With his family's support, Abe had moved to Tokyo after college. He'd had one year left on his dual citizenship and at the time, his dream had been to become an actor. Though he'd been cast in leading roles throughout high school and college without regard to his skin color, finding roles in New York, even with an agent, as an Asian man proved more difficult. One casting director told his agent that Abe was a "Talented actor. Too Asian." Like his genetics were something he should have switched off before walking on stage. He could cry on demand, but the shape and color of his face weren't things he could change. And he didn't want to.

Sure, he'd found roles in Tokyo, but his heart hadn't been in it. The hurried, busy city had been too rushed. Too crowded.

He'd grown up in Boston, but spent his adolescence living just outside Lawrence, Kansas. He was used to wide open green spaces and rolling hills. Abe was used to light traffic conditions even at rush hour and swarming basketball fans in March. But in Tokyo, there were swarms of people, everywhere, all the time. The danger of suffocation was real. Everything closed in on him and crushed him beneath the pressure of so many buildings and bodies.

So, when the year was up, and he'd had to choose, American or Japanese, Abe packed up his few meager belongings and moved back home to Kansas where he could breathe again.

Gretchen elbowed him in the side, and he realized they'd reached the counter. The redhead was at the register while Lane alternated between making coffee and rotating fresh trays of cinnamon rolls and scones out of the oven. After they ordered, they waited at the end of the counter for their cinnamon rolls and Gretchen's mocha, because even the stools at the bar were filled with a line of men around Abe's age.

"Oh my God, those smell so good," Gretchen said as Lane approached with their food.

"I didn't realize you baked too," Abe said. When Lane set the plates with two giant cinnamon rolls down with a bright smile for Gretchen.

Then she turned on her heel and said over her shoulder, "What did you think the ovens were for, genius?"

Gretchen snorted, and Abe pretended he was annoyed, but Gretchen only swiped a finger through the icing on top of her cinnamon roll as Lane returned with Gretchen's coffee. There was a heart swirled into the foam and a sprinkle of cocoa on top.

"Enjoy," Lane said. "I'll be around in a few minutes if you need anything else."

At their table, Gretchen Instagrammed her breakfast before Abe had even sipped his coffee. "I like her," Gretchen said as she traded out her phone for her fork. "How long have you been dating?"

Abe choked on his coffee, too busy spluttering to answer.

"So not long then. She didn't look like she knew about me either."

Abe struggled to pull enough air into his lungs to say, "I'm not dating Lane."

Gretchen looked toward the counter where Lane was chatting with a customer as she iced the newest batch of cinnamon rolls. The redhead had disappeared.

"That's a pretty name," Gretchen said. "There's a Lane a year ahead of me at school, but he's a guy. I like it better for a girl."

"I think it's traditionally a man's name," Abe said.

The heart elongated and distorted as Gretchen took her first sip, a short sigh of relief releasing from her throat. The sound should have come from someone ten years older, who was tired and hung over and needed the heat and the caffeine to recover. For a moment, Abe wondered if "going to the movies with Maddy" had been code for hanging out at Maddy's house and sneaking her parent's liquor, but looking his daughter over, he didn't think so. Gretchen had always been a rule follower. She grew offended and outraged when other people broke the rules, like Lock and Rousseau had been imprinted on her psyche at birth.

She set her mug against her saucer with a clack. "This is the best mocha I have ever had."

Abe didn't bother to hide his chuckle and sipped his own coffee. "Now you see why we're here."

Gretchen tilted her head and narrowed her eyes like she didn't believe him, but he only shrugged. He didn't believe himself either.

Lane was too busy to bother with them as they enjoyed their meal—more sugar than Abe ate in a month—and Gretchen, thankfully, didn't bring up Abe's love life again.

• • • •

THE FOLLOWING TUESDAY, Abe arrived at Cristo's knowing Lane would grill him about never mentioning he had a daughter, that Gretchen had been an unwanted surprise and that it was rude not to prepare her for the introduction. Abe anticipated antagonizing Lane some more, already guessing how many swear words she'd throw at him. But when he sat down, Lane plunked a mug next to his newspaper and swept back to the register with only a sweet-sounding "Good morning."

She ignored Abe in favor of smiling at the young man at the register. She flipped her braid over her shoulder and cocked an eyebrow, chatting with the twenty-something kid like she knew him. The way he pressed his palms into the counter and leaned toward Lane screamed familiarity—possessiveness even.

In that moment, Abe realized he knew nothing about the woman he'd been lusting after for the last month.

Lane possessed a whole life outside his fantasy of her, a whole life outside Cristo's, outside whatever he imagined her schooling was like. This guy might be part of that life. As much as Abe wasn't thrilled about the possibility of Lane having a young, blonde boyfriend, it wasn't any of his business.

As Abe watched the two of them interact, he understood why she'd kept her distance. Lane had said the first morning they'd spoken that she disliked any man who sat on the stool he now sat on. And so far, she'd tolerated him. But he behaved exactly as she expected him to, like she was there for his amusement, just because she was pretty and stuck behind the bar.

Lane didn't want to be watched. She wanted to be seen. She wasn't in the market to take on his baggage. Perhaps she wasn't ready for a family and a house in the country. Perhaps she needed whatever simple connection she had with this young guy.

As Abe watched her take a playful swat at the blonde kid, he wondered if what Lane needed was someone to be her friend. He decided, as she turned her smiling face toward him and their eyes met, just for a moment, it wouldn't be so bad to be her friend either.

Chapter Four

It was well past midnight on Friday when Abe pulled into his garage. The engine of his new Mercedes cut off to reveal the sound of coyotes howling in the distance.

Abe was exhausted. Session was still in full swing, and he wanted a day off, but he'd invited some legislators out for drinks the next night anyway. He should keep working on the house and his long-neglected bedroom in the morning, but as he traversed the footpath between his garage and back porch, he decided he wouldn't.

Abe wanted to spend the day drinking coffee and catching up on last week's unread newspapers. He wanted sit on the big red sofa at Cristo's, away from the guilt and temptation of his unfinished house.

The possibility of seeing Lane sent a jolt of excitement through him. Over the last month, Abe had tried being a customer instead of a suitor. He still sat on his stool, but he ordered coffee and read his newspaper. If Lane had a moment, sometimes they would chat. As a result, Lane's demeanor had softened somewhat, and she told him little things about herself, things like how the knitting needles for one of her final projects were almost too small to see or how she'd spilled indigo all over one of her favorite shirts so she'd dyed the whole damn thing.

Her eyes sparkled like warm embers when she talked about her work, even as he saw her teetering on the edge of exhaustion. He knew it must be hard, juggling a full class load and a full-time job. The subject of her art breathed new life into her, so he asked her about her about it every chance he got. Watching her eyes light, and her lips curl into a smile calmed the usual cold, churning waves in his chest into a smooth Caribbean coastline. He liked how she responded to him now, and he ached to form a deeper connection with her.

Abe shouldn't acknowledge that desire, especially considering where he'd just come from.

Tiffany was nice, but Abe wasn't sure there should be anything serious between them. She was the trainer at his racket club that turned every guy's head. She was blonde and perky. She talked shit on the court and had the power in her backhand to back it up. Tiffany was a single parent, like him, though before tonight he hadn't realized that her son was older than Gretchen.

Carter had been born when Tiffany was nineteen, cutting her off from the pro career she'd been pursuing.

She hadn't seemed sorry as they'd eaten dinner at the new Latin fusion place downtown. She'd chattered about all the competitions she'd won and how Carter already had offers of tennis scholarships from a few schools. Tiffany was strong, funny, and didn't apologize for her confidence—all qualities Abe found attractive. And he had enjoyed his evening.

It was only after, as he was buckling his pants and leaning over to kiss her where she still lay tangled in her sheets that Abe realized they hadn't talked about anything other than sports and their kids. He knew from experience, it wouldn't be enough.

Dread had followed him on the long drive home. It was almost thirty minutes from where Tiffany lived to his little square of land outside Topeka. He shouldn't have slept with her. That much he knew at least, but it had been months and she'd all but pulled him into her bed.

Did that make him a pig?

The connection was physical. The was no disputing that. He felt like an asshole even so. Thinking about Lane only made it worse.

Abe would explore this thing with Tiffany. He'd treat her like a lady, take her out for a few more dates. They would talk more, and if it didn't work out, it wasn't because he'd acted like an animal.

Cristo's was busy the next morning. A sure sign Lane was working. He'd slept late enough that the crowd looked to be on its way out, and Abe snagged a spot on the sofa across from the register just like he'd wanted.

He spent an hour drinking two cups of coffee and catching up on the highlights of the last week's Wall Street Journal and New York Times as the shop cleared out. Though he hadn't done as much reading as he'd planned. Lane moving behind the counter kept distracting him. He watched as she lined up six cups, pulled shots and steamed milk, and mixed every drink while still holding a conversation with whoever was in line next. She should have been a bartender. She'd make a hell of a lot more money.

He'd just been considering ordering a sandwich, since it was lunchtime and he'd skipped breakfast, when Lane plopped into the armchair across from him.

"You're freaking me out," she said, as she crossed an ankle over her knee. Her blue plaid shirt gaped in the front, showing a hint of cleavage despite the black tank top she wore beneath. Abe averted his gaze to the knee-length boots she wore over her jeans instead.

"How's that?" he asked and closed his newspaper to give her his full attention.

"You never sit anywhere but right there." She motioned over her shoulder to the vacant stool closest to the register. "Not when you don't have your daughter with you anyway."

"I thought you didn't like it when men sat there."

Lane shrugged, slouching against the arm chair like she was comfortable with him. The way she said, "I've gotten used to you by now," made Abe's heart rate tick up. What did she mean by that? Did she want him there? "Besides, you, at least, are harmless."

Abe flinched. He might have conflicting emotions about how he wanted Lane to view him, but harmless was not the persona he wanted to project. If she knew how often he'd imagined grasping her round hips and driving between her soft thighs, she would understand how dangerous he could be.

Abe reminded himself that he'd been with Tiffany the night before, and it helped to temper the urge to pull Lane onto his lap and run his tongue up her neck.

God, would he ever stop wondering what she tasted like?

Lane laughed at his flinch. "Sorry to disappoint, but you're the most innocuous counter guy I've had in ages."

"Counter guy?"

"The dudes that all sit on that stool and stare and flirt. You, at least, seem to be here for the coffee and conversation. But today, you only want the coffee, and I'm trying to figure out what's changed."

It was Abe's turn to shrug. "That's easy. I'm seeing somebody."

Lane waggled her eyebrows. "Nice. You needa refill?"

"How about a roast beef sandwich?"

"The one with horseradish or the one with the onions?"

"Horseradish," Abe said. "No cheese."

"Got it."

She disappeared into the kitchen for a few minutes, only to return with a gigantic roast beef sandwich and a side of the spicy pasta salad he'd only ordered once before, but she remembered he'd liked. She even brought a glass of water, no ice.

"Thanks," he said, as he took the food and drink. "Good memory."

"It's my job," Lane raised and lowered her shoulders like it was nothing.

She leaned back in her chair and stretched her arms up over head like she wasn't on the clock. Abe tried not to pay attention to the way her breasts pressed against her apron as he took a bite of his sandwich at the same moment his phone buzzed in his pocket.

The text wasn't from Gretchen like he'd expected, but from Tiffany. It was a pleasant surprise to hear from her so soon.

> **Tiffany:** *Thanks for last night. It was fun.*
> **Abe:** *I had fun too. Are you free Wednesday?*
> **Tiffany:** *I give lessons late on Wednesdays.*
> **Abe:** *Friday? I'd like to take you out again.*
> **Tiffany:** *I don't think so.*

Abe tried to stay optimistic as he typed, *Did I do something wrong?*

> **Tiffany:** *It was fun. And you were great for an Asian guy, but I get the feeling you're a serious commitment kind of guy, and that's just not what I'm looking for right now. I hope that's okay.*

Abe didn't realized Lane was still watching him, or that he'd been scowling at his phone until she asked, "What's wrong?"

Since he didn't have the words to explain, he handed Lane his phone as he washed down the sandwich that had turned to sand in his mouth.

Lane's raised eyebrows creased into a frown as she read. Then one hand covered her mouth as she said, "Holy shit, she did not just say that."

Abe knew which part she meant and nodded. "She did."

"Wow," Lane handed his phone back to him, and he dropped it on the coffee table next to his plate. "And she didn't let on that she was racist as fuck before you slept with her?"

"She's been throwing innuendo at me for months." It was true. Tiffany had flirted since he'd joined the club, and it had only intensified since Christmas. It's why he'd asked her out in the first place. "I'd assumed it wasn't an issue."

"What a bitch," Lane toed the edge of his shoe with her boot. "You deserve better than that."

On the outside, Abe harrumphed and picked up his sandwich. On the inside, he perked up and took notice. Lane not only sought him out, but she touched him. Sure, it was only the sole of her shoe to his, but he'd take the gesture as a sign she didn't count him as one her dreaded counter guys anymore.

The front door chimed, and Lane hopped out of the arm chair with a fluidity that reminded him how much younger she was. The company he usually kept would have grunted and groaned getting up from a chair that low.

The young, blonde kid he now recognized as the guy who worked at the liquor store next door approached the counter. Liquor Store Guy undressed Lane with his eyes, and Abe reminded himself that there was a reason he'd asked someone else out.

Abe couldn't overhear their quiet conversation, but something he'd said had Lane blushing and flipping her braid over her shoulder. It was like watching a train wreck. Abe couldn't look away, because Lane was radiant when she smiled. But she aimed that smile at someone else, someone who looked twenty years younger than Abe. He focused his attention back on his sandwich and newspaper, reminding himself again that he'd decided not to see Lane as anything other than a friend.

It surprised him when, a few minutes later, she pulled the armchair closer to the coffee table and sat down with him again. Without asking, she rifled through his New York Times until she found the *T Magazine*. With a squeak of delight, she crossed her booted feet under her and opened the magazine like a kid with a new comic book.

Abe watched as she flipped through the ads. Every time Lane dogeared a page, for some unknown reason, she would catch her lower lip between her teeth. And though Abe promised himself he wouldn't ask her about her personal life ever, the words slipped out of him as his eyes snagged on her supple pink lips.

"So, is that guy that who just left your boyfriend?"

Lane raised an eyebrow and cocked her head at him. "Shawn?" She released one foot to the floor and adjusted herself in the chair so she faced Abe. "No. Why do you ask?"

"You two seem close, is all."

"He's a friend," Lane's eyes fell back to the magazine. "He likes to flirt, but no. I don't date. Anyone. At all."

Abe wanted to ask why, to tell her she should have fun while she could, that life would catch up to her soon enough and she'd find herself like him, old and alone, but he didn't want to sound patronizing, so instead he said. "Well, your friend watches you like a predator stalking prey, so if you don't date, I'd be careful there."

Lane snorted. "You look at me the same way. So do a lot of guys. It doesn't fucking mean anything."

Abe hadn't meant to touch a nerve. "You're right," he said. "It's none of my business. I'm sorry."

"Yeah, well." Lane stood and held up the magazine. "Can I keep this?"

"Sure," he said, but Lane had already disappeared behind the safety of the counter.

Chapter Five

O ver the course of the next six weeks, Abe went on three more bad first dates. The first was a researcher from the Capitol who'd asked him out, but only talked about policy all evening. The second was a server who'd slipped him her number while he was out to dinner with some legislators. Then there was Denise, a lobbyist who came in from Washington once a year. Though Denise was more of a standing hookup if neither one of them was attached. Last year there had been Nicole, but this year, they'd barely made it through the formality of dinner before she dragged him back to her hotel room.

Abe didn't regret his night, but as he read his newspaper at Cristo's Saturday morning, his eyes more on Lane than the words in front of him, Abe was glad he'd had the dignity not to sleep with the other two. He wouldn't deny that he liked sex, that he needed sex, but he always felt a little dirty the morning after one of his dates as he sat on the sofa at Cristo's and admired Lane.

During the mid-morning lull, Lane had taken to sitting down with him and stealing part of his paper—the arts section or a magazine. They didn't always talk, though sometimes she would point out clothes she'd found in the magazine she thought would suit him. She wasn't wrong. He ordered more than one piece she'd picked out: a pricey sweater and an even more expensive sport coat. The clothes looked good on him, but he didn't have the guts to wear them around her yet.

If he wore the clothes, it would inform her how much power she had over him, and he wasn't ready to tip his cards. He liked the way things stood now, how she talked to him like a friend. It wasn't as satisfying having all that with sex too, but he was happy to settle for the one likely to last longer.

"Are you coming in tomorrow?" Lane asked as she paged through this week's magazine.

"To brunch?"

"Yeah, you haven't been for the last few weeks."

"My daughter likes the waffles at Paradox."

"Hmm," Lane nodded. "A much cooler venue."

"Why do you ask?"

"I wanted to warn you off. I won't be here, so the day will be a disaster."

Abe nodded. She juggled too much of the workload on her own for anyone else to keep up with everything she did. Abe tried to imagine Allison, the red head, moving fast enough to both make drinks and keep the fresh cinnamon rolls coming, but he'd never seen her move like she didn't have weights attached to her limbs.

"Where will you be?" he asked.

"The senior exhibit kicks off tomorrow. There's a reception and everything, so I have to sit in the Spencer all day and wear a dress and explain my art to people."

Abe checked his watch, but the ancient thing didn't display the date. He didn't need the device to tell him it was first weekend in May. Session was almost over. He'd be leaving for vacation soon, one week in Boston with his dad, then one week in Tokyo. While he was gone, Lane would graduate.

"You don't like dresses?"

"I love dresses. It's the explaining part that's useless."

"What are you showing?" he folded his newspaper and sat forward with his elbows on his knees.

Lane flipped a page in her magazine. "Pots and cloth. A couple pieces that incorporate both."

"What kind of pots?" he asked. She said she worked in Japanese forms once upon a time. What did that mean to her?

"Do you mind if I don't talk about it. The whole idea is making me sick to my stomach."

"Whatever you want." Abe sat back and opened his newspaper again with a snap.

"What I want is to sleep for three days straight, and never see this place again, but that's not going to happen."

It had never occurred to Abe before that Lane might not like her job here. She was so professional—aside from the cursing—so efficient at what she did, that he'd just assumed that this was where she wanted to be. He opened his mouth to ask her what she'd want to do instead, but she was already up and bussing the tables on the other side of the shop.

He pulled out his phone and glanced over his schedule for the next two weeks, searching for a spare couple of hours to drive over to Lawrence and spend time wandering around the Spencer Museum of Art at the University of Kansas.

It was Thursday afternoon before Abe made it to Lawrence. Jeff tagged along so they could meet with a Senator from Douglas County on her home turf for dinner. Jeff invited Senator Shepherd along for the outing, who'd been only to keen to accompany them.

Senator Shepherd was young, in her early thirties, and like most politicians from Douglas county, a liberal. They courted her vote on keeping liquor taxes from being a raised on the final budget.

"Oh, I loved art history in college," she said, when Jeff suggested she join them the day before in the Capitol's hallway. "I'd love to go. What are we going to see?" She asked, her brown eyes so focused on Abe that had he not known she was married, he might have mistaken the way she kept looking at him.

Abe didn't want to tell Senator Shepherd, or even Jeff about Lane's art. He said only, "There's a certain piece in a new exhibit I'd like to see."

So, it wasn't until after Abe paid the suggested donation for all three of them and led them into the Senior Exhibit that Jeff looked at him sideways. Senator Shepherd, or Aubrey, as she'd insisted they call her, oohed and ahhed over some abstract sculpture. Jeff got caught up on a series of impressionist style oil paintings with thick, textured brush strokes. Abe only lingered over the ceramic pieces, his eyes searching the attributions for Lane's name.

He realized he didn't even know her last name. If she went only by her initials and her last name, he might never find her.

Abe needn't have worried. He knew Lane's work the moment he saw it. Jeff and Aubrey had meandered on ahead of him and passed right by it. The exhibit's simplicity was almost underwhelming amidst the hard angles and bright colors of the other artist's work. But Lane's work stopped Abe in his tracks.

First, he saw a tiny white teapot with two cups, along with a rectangular serving tray. They all sat on a fabric mat made to look like *tatami*, but that the placard said was woven out of coarse linen. Framing the teapot was one tall and one squat vase, each with silk flowers inside—but not just any silk flowers. The first flower was a lily knit out of silk thread. The second was a peony Lane had woven, then sewn into a flower. Cherry blossom petals, also knit out of silk thread, were sprinkled over the scene. The table was even draped in an indigo fabric with white plum blossoms stamped across the bottom.

Abe snapped a few photos with his phone, photography prohibition be damned. Aubrey and Jeff returned to him as he pocketed his phone.

"Oh, is this what we came to see?" Aubrey asked, her arm brushing against Abe's elbow. He stepped back as she leaned in to read Lane's artist statement. Abe appreciated Aubrey's tenacity, but he would never start an affair with a legislator, much less a married one.

"Oh wow." Jeff clapped Abe on the shoulder. "Lane. That's your barista right?"

Abe only stared at her name on the placard. Lane Benjamin. Then his eyes jumped to where it said each cherry blossom petal took Lane three hours to knit on size quadruple zero needles. Those must have been the needles she'd told him about, the ones she could barely see.

"His barista?" Aubrey asked Jeff.

Jeff chuckled and patted Abe's back before stepping forward to get a closer look at the peony. "Abraham's latest girlfriend. Very pretty, and apparently, very talented."

Aubrey raised her eyebrows at Abe even as she frowned. She didn't need to voice what she was thinking, Abe read the disapproval on her face. A girlfriend in college? Wasn't that a tad too young for him.

"She's just a friend," Abe said. "She mentioned the show, and I was curious. I didn't realize . . ." He motioned toward the piece and trailed off. He'd expected a few pots, maybe some *wabi sabi* tea cups or something—the sort of thing Americans associated

with Japanese art—not the precision in front of him. He wanted
to pick up one of the little cups, to weigh the white clay in his
hand, to run his fingers over the cool glaze.

"Didn't realize what?" Jeff chuckled, the sound too loud in
the whisper quiet gallery. "That you are her exhibit?"

Abe shook his head, his eyes on the fallen cherry petals. He
might have Japanese parents, have family and history in Japan,
but he had chosen to be American. This scene didn't represent
him at all. If Abe wanted to represent himself in art it would a
painting of a churning ocean hung in the middle of his big, unfinished, empty house.

No. This was Lane. The scene was the peace she fought that
fire inside her to achieve. And yet, there existed a sadness in the
scene's placidity that Abe didn't understand.

"Not me," Abe said. "This is Lane."

Both Jeff and Aubrey frowned and reread the artist's statement, which was more about technique than interpretation.
When they didn't see what Abe saw, Jeff turned to Aubrey and
said, "He's been pining after her for months now, but she won't
give him the time of day."

Abe turned on his heel and left the museum, telling himself
he shouldn't have come. All he wanted to do was go to Lane
when he knew he shouldn't.

Chapter Six

Abe didn't go back to Cristo's until after he returned from Tokyo in June. He'd intended to stay away altogether. He'd even made plans with an old friend from law school before he left just so he'd have a date lined up when returned.

Carly had hit him up on Facebook. She was coming back to town for some fundraiser her mother put together. Newly divorced, she needed a date and some company while she contemplated moving back. Would he mind helping an old friend out? He didn't hesitate to accept even though Carly had been more Roxanne's friend than his in law school. They'd gotten along well and stayed more or less in touch since the divorce.

But even with knowing he'd enjoy an evening with an old friend, and the possibility of building on that relationship, Abe didn't stop thinking about Lane. His first Saturday back, Abe went to Cristo's to read his paper like usual, but Lane wasn't there.

The red head worked behind the bar, and instead of the calm, serene vibe that Abe associated with Lane's presence, the atmosphere in Cristo's felt strained. Turmoil churned beneath surface from dissatisfied customers and stale coffee. Abe didn't stay long.

He went home and sanded some of the walls in his bedroom. He called an electrician and scheduled a time for someone to finish the wiring in the bathroom so he could finish the walls and floors in there.

That night, when he donned his tux and picked Carly up for her charity event, he reminded himself that Lane was beyond his reach. She was a woman who didn't date, and even if she did, she didn't want him. So, he donated to the Youth Leadership Project and immersed himself in Carly's beachy blonde waves and slinky red dress until the dancing ended.

They went back to his place since Carly was staying with her mom. She slept with him on the futon in the living room for the next three nights. She cuddled into him while she slept, and practically purred when he ran his fingers over her ribs. She drank too much most nights and liked to smoke up on the balcony after sex. Abe admired her untamable nature, and her refusal to let her divorce get her down.

The stars were bright and the air warm and sticky with residual heat of the day. At Carly's request, Abe had rolled the futon and slung it over his shoulder, hauling it up to the balcony to watch the meteor shower that was supposed to start around midnight.

Exhausted from trying to keep up with Carly's energetic schedule, Abe dozed on the futon. The sickly-sweet smell of Carly's joint anchored him to consciousness.

"We were all so jealous of Roxanne in law school," Carly said.

The mention of his ex-wife stirred him out of his sleep just enough to grunt and wrap his hand around Carly's soft, thin waist.

"I'm serious. You were like, the prize, you know. Mysterious, studious, quiet guy with the smooth voice who was so gorgeous and so aloof."

"I have never been quiet," he said. Starting law school had given him purpose after the aimlessness of Tokyo. "And I wasn't aloof."

"You were that first semester. We all made up stories about where you had come from, and what brought you to Kansas. All of us had strategies about how to get your attention, but the second you met Roxanne, there was zero chance for the rest of us."

Abe dredged up the memories from almost twenty years ago. Roxanne had been the one to talk to him first, though her wild red curls and tall, lithe beauty captivated him the first day of classes. It hadn't been until Thanksgiving that they'd gone out for a drink. They'd gotten married that next August, not even a year after they'd met. They'd been stupid and impractical to get married at twenty-four, in the middle of law school, but they'd done it.

Gretchen came three years later when they were both settling into their careers. Roxanne, still new to the law firm, had barely taken a maternity leave, determined not to fall behind. Instead, Abe had taken a few weeks off work to care for the baby until she was old enough to start daycare. Abe had always known he'd make a good father, had always longed for a large family because his childhood had been so lonely. Those few weeks home with a brand-new Gretchen were some of the best of his life.

Then, only weeks after Gretchen's third birthday, Abe came home from working late to find another man in his bed. Roxanne hadn't even been apologetic about it. She'd been the one to be angry at him. She was always angry at him because he wanted another child, because he wanted her not to exhaust herself at work, because he wanted to take his wife and daughter to meet his family in Japan. Because he didn't take church seriously. Because their daughter preferred him. Because he fixed things around the house instead of hiring someone to do it. Nothing he'd done was enough for her. And he'd resented her for it. He could see that now.

Knowing he'd contributed to her affair didn't take the sharp sting away from knowing she'd chosen someone else instead of coming to him to work things out. He would have tried, if she'd only told him what was wrong.

Carly roused him from his memories when she nuzzled her nose into his ear and said, "These past few days have been like the twenty-three-year-old Carly's dream come true."

He allowed himself to run his finger down her ribcage and over the curve of her slim hip, and she writhed against him. "And what about the forty-year-old Carly?"

"She's realizing that as fun as it is to indulge in a fantasy for a while, there's still a lot of shit for her to wade through back home."

"With your ex?"

"And Mason and Roxy. I thought I wanted to move them here, but as much of a dick as their dad is, it's just not right to move them away from him."

Abe had forgotten she'd named her daughter after Roxanne. They'd been best friends growing up. He shifted against the blankets and looked up at the sky, realizing that whatever fun he'd been having with Carly had just ended.

Chapter Seven

Abe drove Carly to the airport the next morning. It was the least he could do. On the way back to Topeka from Kansas City, Abe decided he was done with women for a while. If someone special came along he'd go for it—someone who kicked him in the gut the way Lane did. Otherwise, he'd concentrate on finishing the house and spending extra time with Gretchen over the summer.

He'd even stay away from Cristo's, because seeing Lane there only made him want to see Lane more the rest of the time.

For two weeks, Abe stuck by his resolve.

One Thursday evening in the middle of July, he'd been invited to a retirement party for a prominent judge. The judge's house was a few miles outside the city limits, just past Cristo's. While Abe didn't want to go, he knew it would be a good networking opportunity.

On the way out of town, he stopped for coffee. He expected to walk away with a cup of lukewarm dregs and a sneer from Allison, but instead Abe found Lane sweeping the floor just inside the door.

She paused her sweeping and cocked her head at him, her fell arms slack with shock.

"Well, hello stranger," she said.

Abe stopped directly in front of her. He'd missed her, and the realization crashed down on him like a tsunami. He'd forgotten how beautiful she was, how her blue eyes sparkled, how her black hair fell over her shoulder in that stupid braid. His fingers itched to pull the rubber band off and unravel the strands until her hair cascaded down her back.

They were alone in the shop. Lane stood less than three feet away from him. The temptation to run his fingers through her hair grew. She might not even protest. The way a little grin tugged at the corners of her mouth, he thought Lane might not mind at all.

"I see how it is now," Lane said when Abe continued to stare at her like an idiot. "You've only been coming around when you think I'm not here." She breezed past him to retrieve her dustpan and tapped his arm with the broom handle. "But the real question, Abraham, is, why have you been avoiding me?"

She was flirting with him. Lane never flirted. She'd joke around sometimes, had even been playful, but anytime he'd tried to flirt, she'd shut him down. Hard.

"Call me Abe," he said. No one called him Abe anymore. He'd gone by it as a child, because Abraham was difficult for his mother to pronounce. She'd been the one to start the nickname, and it's what he'd used all the way through school. He'd gone by Abe until Roxanne. She hated it when people shortened her name to Roxy, and therefore refused to use nicknames.

He'd been Abraham for most of his adult life, but with Lane, he wanted her to use the name his mother used.

Lane kept her eyes on her work as she swept up the pile of dust and coffee grounds. A small, knowing smile played over her lips. His heart sank all the way down into his toes as warmth cascaded over his shoulders.

Lane liked him.

She might not want to, and she might not be ready to admit it, but she was pleased enough to see him that she couldn't hide it. And Abe didn't want to hide what he felt for Lane anymore either.

"Are you still open?" His voice came out hoarse.

"For a few more minutes."

Lane passed him again. She set the broom in the corner and grabbed a spray bottle and a rag off a table close to the bar. "You okay?"

He followed her, half bewitched, to the counter, where they assumed their usual positions. Her leaning next to the cash register behind the bar, him facing her on his stool.

"I'm fine. A little tired."

Abe didn't know what else to say. How did he convey the enormity of what he'd just discovered? The wanting, the desire, the hope for a true connection meant there might be chance for a family. With Lane. For Lane. But he couldn't tell her any of that without scaring her off.

Slow. He'd have to move at a glacier's pace with her.

"There's this drink made out of magic beans that can help with that," Lane said.

"Sounds perfect," he said.

"I'll grab you a cup." Lane warmed two mugs then crossed to the end of the bar and filled them. She set one down in front of him, pulled up her own stool, and took a sip from the other mug. "Now, tell me what you've been up to."

Abe would send cigars and a note to the judge in the morning. He wasn't going to make it to the party.

Keep Reading for a sneak peek of *The Other Lane*

The Other Lane

50

Chapter One

• • • •

CRISTO'S COFFEE HOUSE was a trap—a horrible stinking tar pit of a job that threatened to smother Lane beneath its bubbling surface. It was the worst coffee shop in Topeka, and today, it was competing with itself for its own prize in awfulness. Not only had she stayed up too late, then had to skip her shower because she'd missed her alarm, but Sarah had called in sick. Lane had to balance the phone on her shoulder while steaming milk because she'd had a line out the door all morning. As the cherry on top of her misery sundae, her most obnoxious customer sat on the sofa just opposite the bar, staring at Lane, passing judgment from her ugly thrift store sofa-throne and ignoring her daughter.

It was bad enough that Lane had to serve the pathetic line of middle aged men who perched at the bar to flirt with her, she didn't need an audience. She didn't need an audience who had everything, but liked to spread rumors about which of the suitors was Lane's sugar daddy this week.

Lane shot a glare at the petite, staring woman as she finished the last of the late morning lattes. The heavyset lawyer said goodbye and threw a purposeful dollar bill in the tip jar. The crowd switched from the morning loafers to the lunchtime regulars. A retired couple between rounds of golf looked over their menus. Talia sat with her mom on the sofa, waiting for Talia's dad to join them. When she wasn't looking, Abe sneaked onto the stool the lawyer had just vacated, and was already hiding behind his newspaper.

Abe was the kind of man who knew he was attractive. Tall and lean, he had slick black hair he wore swept back like he had stepped out of the 40s, with a short black beard. Two silver streaks started at his temples and wrapped around like tiger stripes. He wore tailored suits and Lane had made a game out of guessing what color his tie would be. Today it was a dark blue twill.

Close. She'd guessed navy.

The only blemish she'd ever seen on his attire had been the first day he'd visited Cristo's last January. Abe had forgotten to remove the ugly, red Kansas-shaped name tag that identified him as a lobbyist. He had also been wearing a woven silk tie the blue-green color of the ocean that Lane was certain came from an Italian tie-maker she'd studied in school.

She warmed up a mug for his black coffee, then tugged the newspaper down along the center fold just far enough to meet his eyes. He wore a fond, questioning expression that, had she not been used to his beauty by now, might have made her blush and stutter.

"You gonna order something, or you gonna loiter at my counter all day?" she asked.

"Coffee?"

Lane held out the mug. He brushed his fingers against hers for the second day in a row. When Lane narrowed her eyes at him, he winked at her and flashed a cheeky grin. She pretended not to notice, but read his newspaper while he filled his mug. It was the Wichita Eagle that morning. The day before it had been the Hutchinson News.

"How many newspapers do you get?" she asked.

"Four from around the state. Three nationals on Sunday."

She raised an eyebrow. "You read all of those?"

"I compare stories on the same subject by different reporters. The bias changes from paper to paper, region to region."

Lane kept her voice unaffected as she said, "You try so hard to be cool, but you are a huge nerd."

Abe folded his paper with a smirk. "Your hair looks nice like that."

Lane had braided her dirty, tangled hair in a single rope over her shoulder. The black braid reached to her elbow and the tangles were visible through the plaits.

"Nice try," she said. "How was tennis? Did you win today?"

"Won one, lost one—barely."

"I'll bet you're a sore loser."

"Only when I want to win."

"Do you always get what you want?"

"Most of the time." Abe's grin grew wolfish.

Pretending she didn't know what he meant, Lane touched one finger to the square face of his watch, tilting his wrist back just far enough to make out the time. The lunch rush would start any minute. The retired couple was almost finished deciding against the turkey. A big group from the shoe company down the road would show up in a hurry, and Talia and her mom would order the same ham sandwich as always, as soon as her dad showed up.

Lane's gaze lingered on the little girl. She was five, with long black hair. She was adopted, Indian or Pakistani with white parents. Lane had a soft spot for Talia, regularly creating meals that weren't on the menu to make her smile, despite her hatred for her mother.

The smoldering grief that always burned in Lane's chest sparked into flame, sucking all of the air from her lungs.

Abe's fingertips landed on the back of her hand. "You OK?"

Lane snatched her hand off the counter. She searched his face, trying to figure what emotion he'd seen, and if she could pass it off as something mundane.

"My afternoon girl just called in sick. I have to work open to close."

He frowned. "Why can't Allison stay?"

Lane could hear Allison washing dishes in the little kitchen hidden behind the espresso machine. She disappeared whenever one of Lane's suitors showed up, which meant she'd spent most of her morning in the kitchen.

"Because she has afternoon classes."

It hadn't occurred to Lane that she should be upset about working all day. She had work she could do in her studio at home, but that was potential money. Staying to close the shop was six guaranteed hours of overtime money she needed. She should be at home making her art—the art she hoped would some day provide for her living rather than this stupid coffee shop.

"Sit down with me," he said. "I'll buy you lunch."

"I eat for free."

"Then come sit at least."

"You're nuts if you think I'm coming anywhere near you with the rumor mill here." She nodded toward Talia's mom.

Abe looked over his shoulder to see who Lane meant. Just then, Talia's dad entered, still dressed in his pilot's coveralls. He kissed his wife and scooped up his daughter, spinning her in two tight circles.

"Cute family though," he said.

"Almost makes me miss being married," Lane said.

Abe rotated around to face her with a surprised lift of his brow.

Lane covered her mouth. "Shit."

"You were married?"

She nodded, her heart pounding.

"And you were keeping it a secret because?"

"I don't talk about my personal life with customers."

Abe pretended she'd wounded him, placing one long-fingered hand over his chest. "We're pals," he said. "You know all about me."

"Not by choice."

Once upon a time, he'd regaled her with the adventures that were his frequent and awful first dates. Recently though, he hadn't shared any awkward dinner conversations or self-deprecating post-coital stories about how he was good, for an Asian guy.

"What happened? Are you widowed? Divorced?"

Lane swallowed. She wasn't getting out of it now. "Divorced."

"Why didn't you tell me?" he asked. "Was it bad?"

"I'm not talking about this," she said.

"Is that why it took you so long to finish school?"

Lane had only earned her bachelor's degree the previous spring, taking five years longer than most of her classmates.

She wanted to ask him how old he thought she was, but that would only encourage him, and she did not want to talk to him about this.

"I'm not your pal," she said. "I'm your barista."

"Lane." Abe reached over the counter for her hand, but Lane backed out of reach, shaking her head.

"Off limits, Fujikawa."

The large party she'd been expecting walked in, and Abe retreated behind his newspaper. By the time she was free, he had gone. On the counter in his place was enough money to pay for his coffee three times over.

As Lane folded the extra bills into the tip jar, she watched Talia's mom mime Abe and Lane's exchange over the newspaper to her husband.

· · · ·

BY SEVEN O'CLOCK, LANE was so tired and angry that she wanted to spit fire. The ladies Bible study had arrived at half past five, bringing Talia's mom into the shop for the second time that day. She and a friend had stayed after Bible study to gossip. Lane overheard her say she hadn't ordered coffee because she'd read it made you fat. Then she had looked Lane right in the eye. Lane, who was counting down the drawer early, cursed the woman under her breath. She didn't consider herself overweight, she also didn't understand the other woman's need to antagonize her. And, even if she did carry a few extra pounds on her hips and over her belly, Lane liked the way she looked.

The front door opened with a bang. Lane startled and lost count as Javier swaggered in. The middle aged, portly man with slicked back, greasy hair owned the Mexican restaurant on the corner. He wore cheap, outdated suits as if they were James Bond's finest.

"What are you still doing here, Beautiful?" he asked, seating himself at the stool closest to the cash register.

"How many times have I told you to stop calling me that?" Lane asked. She poured the milk for his latte without asking what he wanted.

"But you are beautiful," Javier said, affecting a South American accent. He liked to pretend that he was from South America like some of his cooks, but he'd been born and raised in Kansas.

"You can cut the crap. I have been here since open, I know I look like shit," Lane said when she set his large latte down in front of him. Her comment earned her a glare from the church ladies, but Javier laughed.

"You wouldn't have to work double shifts if you were my bartender," Javier said.

"If I had any desire to serve weak beer and cheap margaritas, I could find a better joint than yours to do it in," Lane said.

Javier had been teasing her about becoming his bar manager for a year now. He was as stingy as he was sleazy and each offer to come work for him was tinged with a side of adultery.

"You should come over and have a drink when you get off," he said. "You deserve it."

"And risk the wrath of your wife?" Lane said. "Not a chance."

"My wife is scary as hell, That's why I come over here."

"Yeah, well, I'm about to close, so you're going to have to head back over to your place and face her." Lane held her hand out for his money.

He pulled out his thick wallet and rifled through the bills inside. "How much is it again?"

"Five even. Same as it was this morning."

"You're robbing me," he said.

"Order a smaller drink."

He held out a five, and Lane tried to take it, but he firmed his grasp on the bill at the last second, tugging it back out of Lane's hand. He played this game every time he paid. This time, she snatched the five out of his fingers. His hand shot out and he grabbed Lane around the wrist, closing his fingers so hard it hurt.

Lane froze as he tightened his grip.

He watched her, wearing a lewd grin.

"Mr. Vasquez," she said, "you need to let go of me."

Talia's mom and her friend were staring at Javier's hand on Lane's wrist. He looked over his shoulder at them and smiled. It was fine, he told them, he and Lane knew each other. They were pals.

He let go of Lane's arm, and she withdrew to cash register.

"Closing time," she said. "Everyone out."

Javier harrumphed, but as he backed out the front door, he blew Lane a kiss. "Goodnight, Beautiful."

Lane ran a finger over the red hand print on her arm as she waited for the two women to gather their things.

Talia's mom gave Lane an appraising look as she walked them to the door. "You know, if you didn't encourage those guys, this kind of thing wouldn't happen so often."

Lane smiled and held the door open for them. "Thanks for coming. I'll see you tomorrow," she said.

She finished her cleaning quickly, and the familiar process calmed her. Exhaustion settled in as she hauled the trash out to the dumpster, and she hoped the pain in her feet would dull enough to let her get some sleep.

Lane stopped in the bathroom to check her reflection in the mirror before she left. Her hair was frizzy, so she brushed her fingers through it and redid the braid. The tiny stud in her nose winked in the artificial light, but Lane only saw the dark circles under her eyes and the contrasting paleness of her complexion.

Javier wasn't the only one who gave her a nickname that implied she was pretty. Her sharp jaw and high cheek bones were softened by subtle dimples in her cheeks, and her blue eyes were large and bright. She was curvy and soft. While she found her contours pleasing, most of the time, she tried to camouflage them with too-big thrifted men's shirts. But Lane wanted to be noticed. She opened an extra button on her shirt and dug in her bag for a tube of lip gloss. She rolled down her sleeves to cover the fading hand print, hoping it wouldn't bruise.

There were no customers in the liquor store when Lane limped in. A football game droned from the TV over the beer case. Shawn was typing so intently at his computer he didn't notice her at first.

"Hey," she said, and he looked up, adjusting his faded blue ball cap. Too preoccupied with whatever story he was currently writing to spend much time on his appearance, Shawn's overgrown, honey blonde hair curled around his hat. His button down shirt and holey jeans were shabby, but his skin still glowed golden from his summer tan.

"Hey, Gorgeous," he said, "What are you still doing here?"

Lane leaned on the counter, trying to take some of the pressure off her sore feet. "Sarah called in sick."

"That's bullshit."

"And so were the tips," Lane said into the countertop. "So I need a bottle of wine that costs less than twelve dollars."

"Red or white?" Shawn asked.

"Now, you know I'm not a white wine kind of girl." She was so tired, it was the only joke she could muster.

"Right. We got a new brand of cab. It has a hedgehog on the label, so it'll be around for about five minutes."

"How much?"

"Nine bucks."

"Sold," Lane said, but did not move.

"You want me to get that for you?" He asked.

"If you don't mind." Lane slid down the front of the counter until she was a heap on the floor. "Is it OK if I sit here for a few minutes?"

Shawn retrieved the wine and joined her. She lay her head on his shoulder and he rested a hand on her thigh. The heat of his palm melted through her jeans.

"Stay as long as you like. It's been dead all evening."

She closed her eyes and listened to the football game. "How do you write with this garbage going?"

"I don't even notice it anymore."

"It would drive me crazy."

"I can write through almost anything."

"It's your superpower."

"I like to think I have a couple of superpowers." Shawn squeezed her leg.

Lane knew what he meant. "Want to come over?" she asked.

"I suppose I could let you feed me soon."

"Is that all I'm good for?"

Shawn took her hand. "You know I think you're amazing. It's our damn schedules that get in the way."

"Are you free tonight?"

"I've got papers and homework," he said. "I could come over after my shift next Friday."

"So long?"

"It's all I've got. Take it or leave it."
"You know I'll take it," Lane said.

For sneak peeks of my latest books and the upcoming deals (including free books!)

Sign up for my newsletter
BookHip.com/STTWHS[1]

Now Sampling Chapters 1-3 of *Sparkle & Shine,* book two of the Try Again series with every sign up

---

1. https://bookhip.com/STTWHS

Other books by Marla Holt out now:
The Other Lane: A Modern Fairy Tale
Ethan & Juliet, Try Again Series, Book 1

• • • •

Coming in 2019:
Sparkle & Shine, Try Again Series Book 2
Read & Wright, Try Again Series Book 3
The Lightning Crashes Duet

About the Author

Marla Holt grew up wishing the heroines in the fairy tales she loved had more to choose from than marrying the prince or utter devastation, so now she writes modern day fairy tales with a feminist flare. She's living her own dream come true, writing and knitting in Topeka, Kansas with her husband and three boys.

Read more at tinydinostudios.com.